CONTENTS

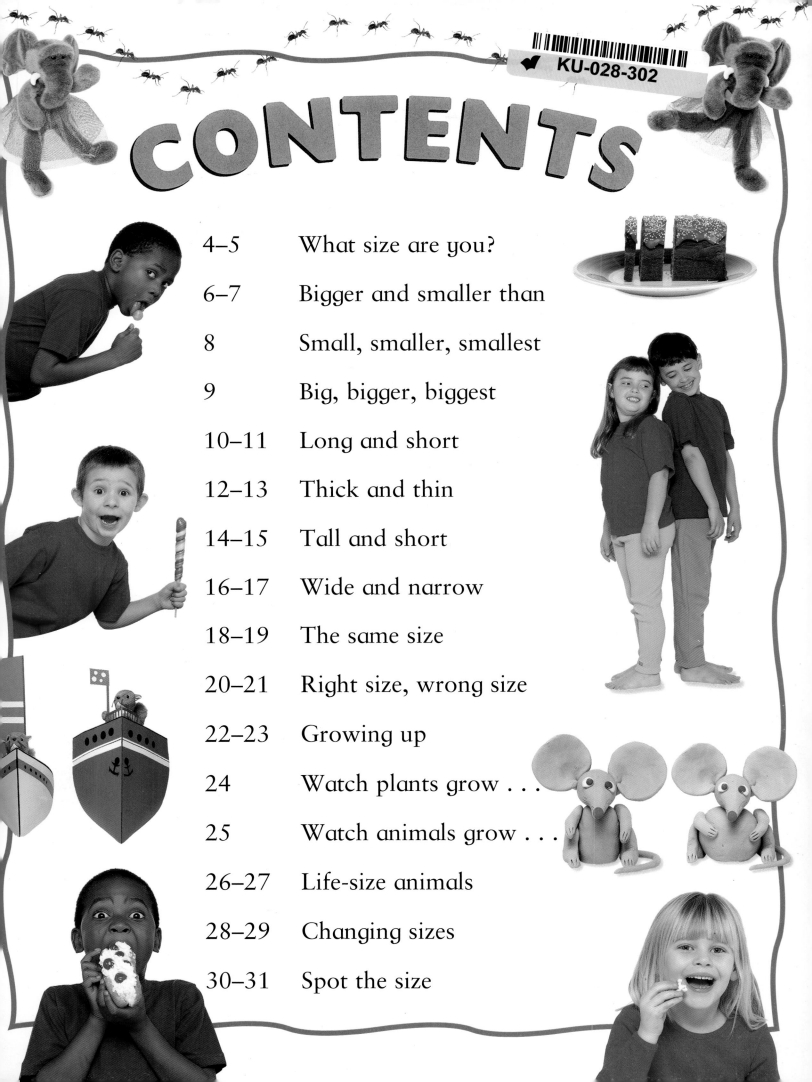

What size are you?

Tall, short, little, big – all of us have the same sort of shape, but we come in many different sizes.

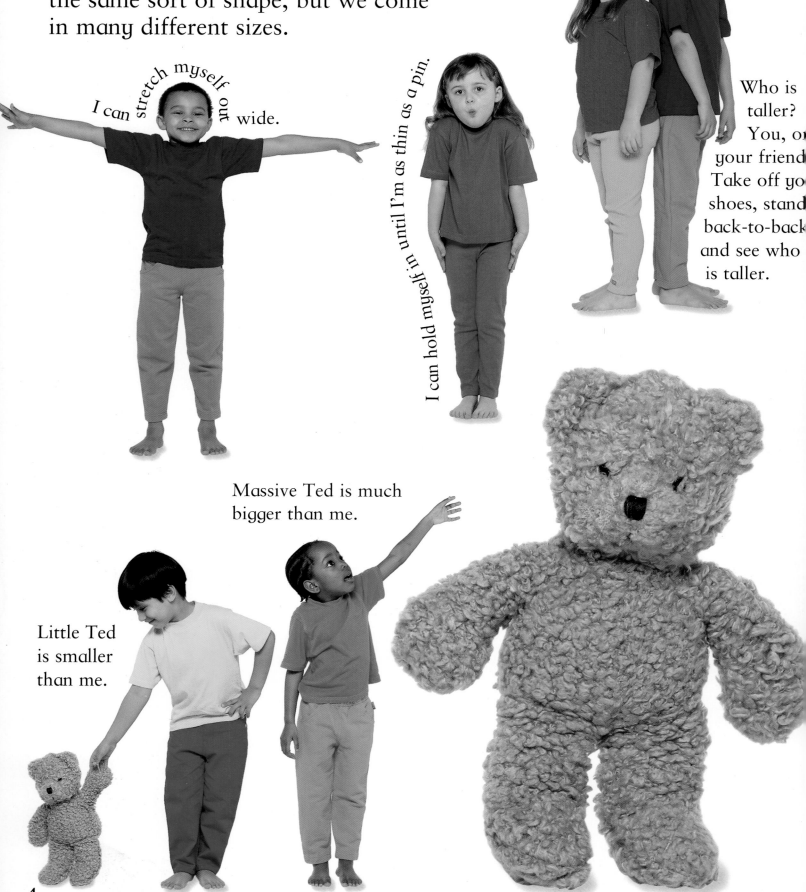

I can stretch myself out wide.

I can hold myself in until I'm as thin as a pin.

Who is taller? You, or your friend? Take off your shoes, stand back-to-back and see who is taller.

Massive Ted is much bigger than me.

Little Ted is smaller than me.

4

PLAYSCHOOL

Sizes

Claire Llewellyn

Educational Consultant: Dr Naima Browne

southwater

NOTES

Fun to Learn Sizes introduces children to the concept of size. Lively pictures and stimulating activities encourage them to understand and compare the differences between sizes.

Learning the basics
This book shows children that size is one of the ways in which we group things. Matching, sorting and classifying are important concepts. They lie behind the mathematics covered in the first year of school.

Reading together
You can help your child by reading aloud the words that accompany the pictures. Go through the book at your child's pace, looking at a couple of topics at a time. Allow plenty of time to talk about the ideas before moving on to talk about others. This way, reading times are enjoyable.

Talking it through
Help your child's understanding by encouraging them to talk about the pictures and relate what they see to their own experiences. This will help your child to develop self-confidence and make the ideas meaningful.

Learning by doing
Encourage your child to try the activities. They can help to extend and develop skills further. Try to make everyday activities an adventure in learning – tidying a wardrobe or going to the supermarket offer plenty of opportunities to talk about size.

Checking your child's understanding
Check your child's understanding of size by asking useful questions about everyday activities. For example, when you are laying the table for a meal you could ask – Which spoons are the biggest? Which glasses are the same size? Always remember to praise your child.

My legs don't stretch very far yet.

My legs are longer.

I have the longest legs of all three.

When you do a forward roll . . .

you go from tall . . .

to a small, tight ball.

Stretch up tall . . .   bend your knees . . .   crouch right down . . .   and tuck in your head.

Is your hair . . .

short . . .

long, . . .

or in-between?

Bigger and smaller than

Look around you each day to spot people, places and things that are bigger or smaller than each other.

An Afghan hound is much bigger than . . .

a Yorkshire terrier.

enormous present

smaller present

big rabbit ears

smaller cat's ears

My small lollipop will soon be gone.

My bigger lollipop will last all day long.

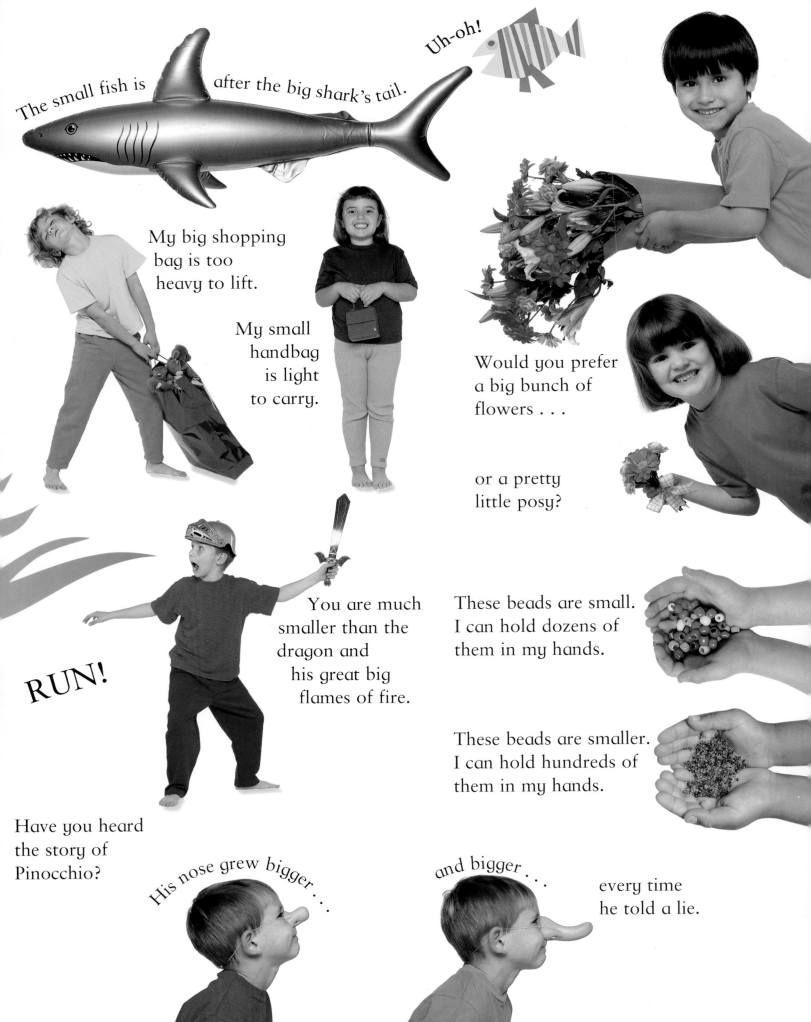

The small fish is after the big shark's tail. Uh-oh!

My big shopping bag is too heavy to lift.

My small handbag is light to carry.

Would you prefer a big bunch of flowers . . .

or a pretty little posy?

RUN!

You are much smaller than the dragon and his great big flames of fire.

These beads are small. I can hold dozens of them in my hands.

These beads are smaller. I can hold hundreds of them in my hands.

Have you heard the story of Pinocchio?

His nose grew bigger . . .

and bigger . . .

every time he told a lie.

Small, smaller, smallest

We sort small things in order of size: small, smaller and the smallest of them all.

small ladybird

smaller ladybird

smallest ladybird

Small peas always seem to taste the sweetest.

Which frog has the smallest parachute?

Three mice sailing across the salty sea.

Try this!

Make three-size cookies

1. Buy some ready-made cookie dough. Find three cutters of different sizes.

2. Roll the dough flat with a rolling pin.

3. Cut out the biscuits with the three cutters.

4. Bake in the oven until they are golden brown in colour.

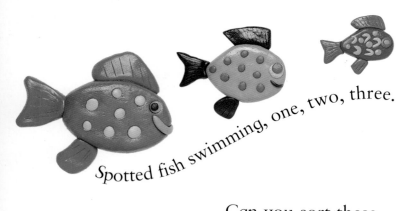
Spotted fish swimming, one, two, three.

Can you sort these hats in order of size?

Big, bigger, biggest

Spot the **biggest** ballerina . . .

Long and short

Can you sort long things from short things?
Look at the objects on this page, then try
to find others at home.

short-tailed lizard

long-tailed lizard

Here is a short line of elephants queuing for a bus.

A super heroine
can fly off quickly
in a short cape.

A king walks
slowly in a
long cloak.

The bus has not arrived yet and the short queue has become a long one.

Short socks cover
my ankles.

Long socks almost
reach my knees.

Yum! Yum!

If you had a choice of long, slurpy
spaghetti strands or short pasta bows,
which would you want to eat?

Try this!

Make a slinky snake

1. Get nine paper cups and paint them.

2. Take a cup for the head. Stick an eye on it.

3. Using a pencil, carefully make a hole in the bottom of the cup.

4. Thread string through the hole and tie a knot.

5. Join the cups together with paper fasteners.

Pull your slinky snake along.

Most cats have long tails, but the Manx cat has a short, stubby one.

long neck

If my neck was as long as a giraffe's, I could see high above the trees.

short neck

Did you know?

The giraffe's neck is longer than any other animal's.

Will you grow a moustache when you are older?

Will your hair be long or short?

11

Thick and thin

Would you choose the thick or thin things on this page? Is one better than the other?

Two monkeys are swinging on ropes.

Hey!

Help yourself to a piece of cake. Which slice would you like?

Which rope do you think will break?

Look at me!

Did you know?

Polar bears have thick fur coats to keep them warm in the cold.

The wizard's thick book of magic is full of weird and wonderful spells!

The teds' book is thinner. It won't take long to read.

How shall I wear my hair . . .

in two thick plaits . . .

or in lots of thin plaits?

Which spiders have the thickest legs?

12

A thick jumper warms you up on cold days.

A thin T-shirt keeps you cool on hot days.

Frog and Squirrel are painting.

Are their paintings the same?

A thick rubber ring will help you to float in water.

Can you spin a hula-hoop around your waist?

Would you rather munch on a very thick sandwich or a very thin one?

Try this!

Thick and thin sandwiches

1. Ask an adult to cut four slices of bread – two thick and two thin. Butter them.

2. Ask for two slices of cheese – one thick and one thin.

3. Now ask for four slices of cucumber – two thick and two thin.

4. Make one very thick and one very thin sandwich.

thick sandwich   thin sandwich

Tall and short

There are tall and short things all around us in the house, in the street, in the park. Which ones can you name?

Are you taller than your teddy bear?

Which of these towers has more beakers?

We need a taller ladder to rescue Chicken from the tower. This short ladder will not reach to the top.

A pudding is a delicious treat. Which one would you choose to eat?

14

Try this!

Who wears a hat?

1. Think of two people who wear hats. Draw them on a piece of paper.

2. Now think about their hats. Are they tall or short? Draw them on the picture.

3. Colour in your pictures with felt-tip pens or crayons.

Pull out the sides of a bendy mirror and it will make you look short. Push on the sides and you will look taller.

Look at these two teddy bear towers. Which one is taller?

Can you spot any differences between these two hats?

a tall blade of grass

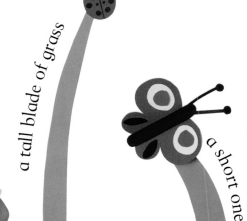

a short one

15

Wide and narrow

Spotting whether things are wide or narrow is a way of seeing how much space they take up.

wide sunglasses   narrow sunglasses

wide tie   narrow tie

Stretching out to walk through a wide gap.

Squeezing through a narrow gap.

A mouse hole is wide enough for a tiny mouse but too narrow for a fat cat!

Which is the wide boat and which is the narrower boat?

wide blue sea

A big car needs four wide tyres.

A skinny bike only needs two narrow tyres.

Lots of narrow bangles will easily fit on your arm.

How many wide bangles will fit on your arm?

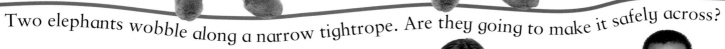

Two elephants wobble along a narrow tightrope. Are they going to make it safely across?

Spiders scuttle along a wide plank.

Some ribbons are wide and silky. Others are narrow and fine.

Would you choose to wear . . .

narrow, clingy leggings . . .

or wide, baggy trousers?

Hip-hip-hooray!

For an eye-popping finale . . . stretch your arms out as wide as you can.

17

The same size

Two socks, two shoes, two gloves –
when two things are the same size,
we say that they make a pair.

A clown's shoes

Two shoes in the same size make a pair.

Ted is balancing
on a pair of skis.

Now he can slide
down the snowy
mountain slope.

A scooter has
two wheels
that are just
the same size.

Make sure that
your roller skates
are the same size!

Some musical instruments come in pairs.

Crassh!

Crassh!

You need
two cymbals
to make a
loud noise.

Shake your maracas
gently for a soft
sound or hard
for a loud one.

T sshh

T sshh

Whose shoes?

A pair of shoes that tinkle and curl.
Who can they belong to?

Glittery party shoes

A perfect fit! The prince has finally found his princess.

Two cold hands need two woolly gloves.

Do you think these gloves will fit?

Look at yourself closely in the mirror.

You have two eyes and two ears just the same size.

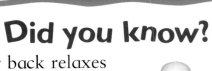

What other parts of your body are the same size?

Did you know?

Your back relaxes and stretches out while you are sleeping at night. So when you wake-up you are a little bit taller than you were the day before.

19

Right size, wrong size

It's important to have some things just the right size. You cannot ride a bike that is much too big, or wear shoes that are too small.

Are these children wearing the right-sized clothes?

This chair is the right size.

Oops! This one isn't.

Try this!

Make a paper doll

1. Draw a paper doll. It can be anything you want - an animal or a girl or a boy.

2. Lay see-through paper over the drawing. Draw some clothes for the doll.

3. Cut out the clothes and stick them on the doll. Do they fit?

Can you eat a cream cake in just one bite?

A small mouthful of cheese is just about right.

A piece of popcorn is the right size and tastes just as nice.

These shoes are the wrong size for me . . .

. . . but these shoes fit perfectly.

Did you know?

You need to be measured to know which clothes and shoes are the right size for you.

Two teddy bears are going for a ride.

Who has the right-sized bike?

Which suitcase is the right size for you?

too big

too small

The wrong-sized toothbrush.

Who is wearing the wrong-sized glasses?

The right-sized toothbrush.

21

Growing UP

Our body changes as we get older. We grow taller and wider and we need bigger and bigger things.

A one-year-old baby can crawl.

A three-year-old toddler can walk and run.

An eight-year-old child can do things f-a-s-t!

Babies grow out of their clothes very quickly.

Toddlers learn how to dress themselves.

A bigger child needs bigger clothes.

A baby wears slippers to keep its feet warm.

A toddler's shoes slip on and off easily.

How old were you when you first tied your shoelaces?

Some babies are carried in safety chairs like this.

How old do you think the owner of this tricycle is?

Stabilizers will help you balance when you learn to ride a bike.

A 13-year-old teenager is tall and strong.

At 25, you may have stopped growing!

Try this!

See how you grow

1. Hang a big piece of paper on the wall. Stand in front of it and ask a friend to draw around you.

2. When you step away from the paper, the drawing will show the shape of your body.

Whose shirt is this?

Do you like to wear fashionable clothes?

3. Do the same thing one month later. Ask your friend to draw around you in a different colour.

Trainers are comfortable and easy to walk in.

High-heeled shoes are harder to walk in.

4. Take a ruler and measure the difference between the two body shapes. Have you grown?

Only adults are allowed to ride a motorbike.

When you are older, you can ride on the road.

watch it grow...

Plants and animals are living things, too. Like people, they start life small but, as long as they have plenty of food, they soon begin to grow.

Small acorns grow on oak trees.

They fall to the ground in autumn and grow in the spring.

The young tree grows leaves in its first year.

20 years later, the oak tree is as tall as a house, and still growing!

Try this! Grow some sprouts

1. Soak some mung beans in water overnight. Drain them and leave in a covered jar.

2. After two days, the beans will start to sprout. Sprinkle them on top of a salad and serve.

Watch animals grow...

Baby animals grow more quickly than humans. In just a couple of months, they may be ten times bigger than when they were born.

When kittens are born their mother licks them clean.

Even after one week a kitten's eyes are still tightly closed.

At three weeks, the kitten has started to move around. But it is still not very strong.

Nine weeks old, and the kitten is almost ready for its first trip outside.

This puppy is three days old. It only sleeps and eats.

Three weeks old, and the puppy is becoming more active.

At five weeks puppies begin to be curious about the world around them.

After eight weeks the puppies are ready to go to a new home.

This baby owl is resting after hatching out of its shell.

A group of two-week-old owlets wait for a meal.

Four weeks old, and the owlets are moving around their nest.

After twelve weeks an owlet loses its fluffy feathers and is growing fast.

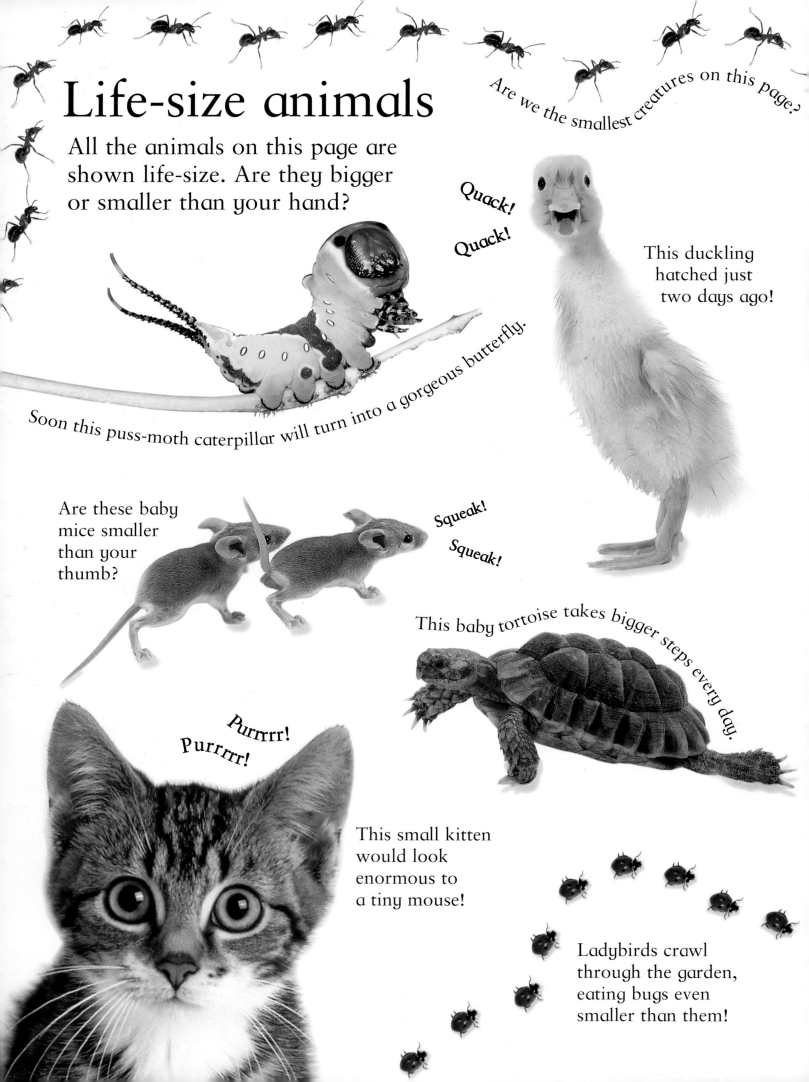

Life-size animals

All the animals on this page are shown life-size. Are they bigger or smaller than your hand?

Are we the smallest creatures on this page?

Quack! Quack!

This duckling hatched just two days ago!

Soon this puss-moth caterpillar will turn into a gorgeous butterfly.

Are these baby mice smaller than your thumb?

Squeak! Squeak!

This baby tortoise takes bigger steps every day.

Purrrrr! Purrrrr!

This small kitten would look enormous to a tiny mouse!

Ladybirds crawl through the garden, eating bugs even smaller than them!

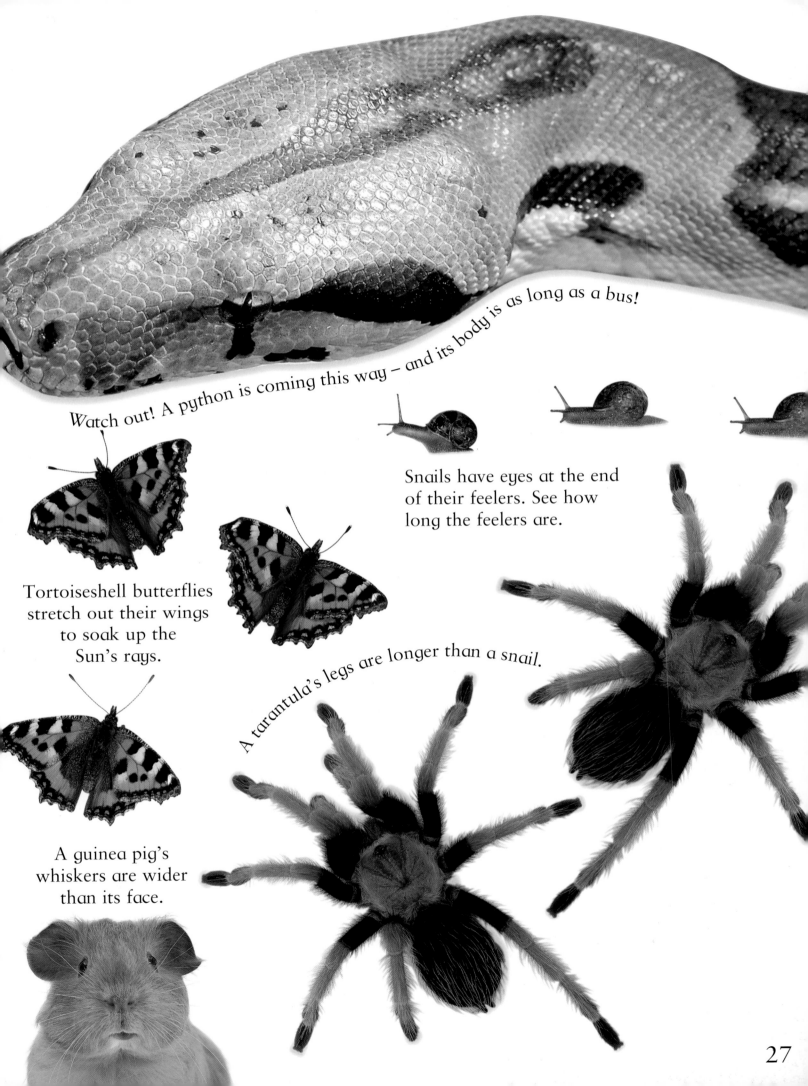

Watch out! A python is coming this way – and its body is as long as a bus!

Snails have eyes at the end of their feelers. See how long the feelers are.

Tortoiseshell butterflies stretch out their wings to soak up the Sun's rays.

A tarantula's legs are longer than a snail.

A guinea pig's whiskers are wider than its face.

27

Changing Sizes

How can you change the size of something?
By stretching or shrinking it, or puffing it
up, or breaking it into bits!

You can build a big
castle with lots of
little bricks .

Break a big bar of chocolate
into little squares and share
them with your friends.

My T-shirt
is too small
for me now.
It must have
shrunk in
the wash.

Yum! Yum!

Oh dear!

I am hungry.

Now I am full.

You need a
lot of puff
to blow up
a balloon.

Puff, puff!
It is
getting
bigger.

Puff, puff!
Now it
is even
bigger.

My skirt has an elastic waist. It fits me perfectly. Or it can stretch and stretch to make room for two.

A small amount of cake mixture becomes a big cake after it is cooked.

Can you put all the pieces of a jigsaw puzzle together?

Pop!

Now it is the same size as when I started.

Try this!

Make a picture puzzle

1. Draw a picture on a piece of thin card. Colour it brightly.

2. On the back, draw four or five wiggly lines across the card.

3. Cut the card into pieces along the lines.

4. Ask a friend to put the puzzle pieces back together again.

29

Spot the size

Take it in turns to throw the dice and move your counter around the board. When you land on a square, look for the answers on the page. You have ten seconds to do this. If you can't, you miss a turn. If you can, you have another go. The first one to finish is the winner.

You will need 2 counters or buttons, a timer and a dice.

START

1 Find another ladybird of the same size.

2 Just how big can his nose grow? Find an even bigger one.

3 Find me with my blown-up balloon.

4 I've got thin legs. Find the spider with thicker legs.

10 Find someone with a short moustache.

9 Find a wide bangle.

5 Find the smallest frog.

6 Find a lizard with a long tail.

7 Find a tall pudding.

8 Find a bigger ted.

30

13

Find a shorter tower.

14

Find a longer blade of grass.

15

I was thinner before I ate that cheese. Where is the thinner me?

11

Find a thicker sandwich.

12

Find the same size boot.

16

Find a narrower boat.

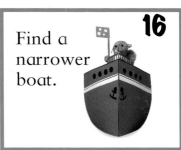

17

Find an older kitten.

FINISH

21

Find someone who is stretching out wide.

20

These shoes are too big – find me a pair that will fit properly.

19

Find the wrong-sized toothbrush.

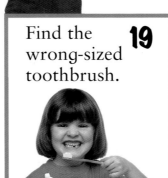

18

Whoops! Elephant has sat on the wrong chair. Find the right-sized chair for him.

This edition is published by Southwater
Southwater is an imprint of Anness Publishing Ltd, Hermes House, 88–89 Blackfriars Road, London SE1 8HA
tel. 020 7401 2077; fax 020 7633 9499; www.southwaterbooks.com; info@anness.com
© Anness Publishing Ltd 1999, 2002

Published in the USA by Southwater, Anness Publishing Inc., 27 West 20th Street, New York, NY 10011;
fax 212 807 6813

This edition distributed in the UK by The Manning Partnership Ltd, 6 The Old Dairy, Melcombe Road, Bath BA2
3LR; tel. 01225 478 444; fax 01225 478 440; sales@manning-partnership.co.uk

This edition distributed in the USA by National Book Network, 4720 Boston Way, Lanham, MD 20706; tel. 301 459
3366; fax 301 459 1705; www.nbnbooks.com

This edition distributed in Canada by General Publishing, 895 Don Mills Road, 400–402 Park Centre, Toronto,
Ontario M3C 1W3; tel. 416 445 3333; fax 416 445 5991; www.genpub.com

This edition distributed in Australia by Pan Macmillan Australia, Level 18, St Martins Tower, 31 Market St, Sydney,
NSW 2000

This edition distributed in New Zealand by The Five Mile Press (NZ) Ltd, PO Box 33–1071 Takapuna, Unit
11/101–111 Diana Drive, Glenfield, Auckland 10; tel. (09) 444 4144; fax (09) 444 4518; fivemilenz@clear.net.nz

Publisher: Joanna Lorenz
Managing Editor, Children's Books: Linda Fraser
Project Editor: Joanne Hanks
Educational Consultant: Dr Naima Browne
Design: Tessa Barwick
Photography: John Freeman
Stylist: Melanie Williams

Previously published as *Fun to Learn: Sizes*

The Publishers would like to thank the following children for appearing in this book: Josh Atkins, Daisy Bartlett,
Callum Brooks, Andrew Brown, April Cain, Milo Clare, Alice Crawley, Ruben Fox, Luke Fry, Africa George, Safari
George, Jerome Gerard, Zaafir Ghany, Miriam Nadia Halgane, Jackson Harrington, Madison Harrington, Faye
Harrison, Jasmine Haynes, Joseph Haynes, Rhys Hillier, Kadeem Johnson, Zamour Johnson, Sumaya Khassal, Rosa
Linchnorthover, Otis Lindblom Smith, Caroline Marin de Silvia, Lucy Martin, Holly Matthews, Rebekah Murrell,
Lucie Ozanne-Martin, Philip Quach, Lateef Saka, Jason Sosa, Tom Rawlings, Grace Updon, James Xu

1 3 5 7 9 10 8 6 4 2